P9-CDZ-947

WITHDRAWN

An Undone Fairy Tale

by Ian Lendler

illustrated by Whitney Martin

KERSHAW COUNTY LIBRARY
632 W. DeKalb St. Suite 109
Camden, South Carolina 29020

Simon & Schuster Books for Young Readers
NEW YORK   LONDON   TORONTO   SYDNEY

SIMON & SCHUSTER BOOKS FOR YOUNG READERS
An imprint of Simon & Schuster Children's Publishing Division
1230 Avenue of the Americas, New York, New York 10020
Text copyright © 2005 by Ian Lendler
Illustrations copyright © 2005 by Whitney Martin
All rights reserved, including the right of
reproduction in whole or in part in any form.
SIMON & SCHUSTER BOOKS FOR YOUNG READERS
is a trademark of Simon & Schuster, Inc.
Book design by Dan Potash.
The text for this book is set in Rochambeau.
The illustrations for this book are rendered in watercolor and gouche.
Manufactured in China
4 6 8 10 9 7 5
Library of Congress Cataloging-in-Publication Data
Lendler, Ian.
An undone fairy tale / Ian Lendler ;
illustrated by Whitney Martin.—1st ed.
p. cm.
Summary: When its illustrator cannot keep up
with its reader, a story about a selfish, pie-loving
king takes numerous silly detours.
ISBN 0-689-86677-1 (ISBN-13: 978-0-689-86677-7) (hardcover)
[1. Fairy tales. 2. Kings, queens, rulers, etc.—Fiction.
3. Princesses—Fiction. 4. Humorous stories.]
I. Martin, Whitney, 1968– ill. II. Title.
PZ8.L47695 Un 2005
[E]—dc22   2003016390

This book is dedicated to Gonzo the Great, a true comic genius—I. L.

For my mom, Beverly A. Martin, for encouraging me
to be an artist from the start—W. M.

Acknowledgments
This book wouldn't exist without Kusum's initial giggle, Jason's
endless editing, Deirdre's invaluable advice, Tanya's golden eye,
David's guiding hand, and Whitney making it look real purty.—I. L.

I would like to thank Teresa for all of her patience, support, and
understanding; John Mahoney for his friendship and creative inspiration;
Barbara Bradley for helping me learn how to draw; Walt Stanchfield for his
enthusiastic love of art and teaching; Ian Lendler for such a fun manuscript;
and Dan Potash for giving me a shot at all of this.—W. M.

Once upon a time there lived a princess who was famous throughout the land. Not only was she beautiful, but she baked the most delicious pies in the kingdom. Many men wished to marry her. But she was very lonely.

You see, her stepfather, the king, loved her for only one reason—her pies.

And to keep anyone else from having them, he locked her in a tall, dark tower.

No one, not even her mother, could help her.

Every day the princess had to bake pies for the new king. And every night she prayed to be rescued.

Many knights tried. But before they could marry the princess, the king made each knight perform three dangerous tasks. All of them failed.

And as she watched the days and knights pass, the princess gave up hope.

Until one day . . .

Sir Wilbur arrived—the bravest, most famous knight around. He told the king, "Your Highness, I wish to marry your daughter."

You may have noticed the king's unusual crown. Let me explain. You see that fellow painting the wall? That's Ned. Wave hi, Ned!

He's making all the pictures for this story. But you're reading so quickly that he hasn't finished the painting or the costumes for this page yet. So instead of a crown, he just stuck a doughnut on the king's head. We'll pretend that's a crown though, okay? Good.

The king said, "For your first task, you must slay the savage dragon that threatens our land."

Sir Wilbur said, "It shall be done. Fetch my horse and armor!"

Sorry to interrupt again, but you're still reading very fast. Please don't turn the page. Ned doesn't have the horses or armor yet.

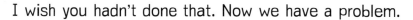

I wish you hadn't done that. Now we have a problem.

Sir Wilbur and his men need to ride something, and all Ned has are these fish. And the only costumes ready are these tutus. But since you kept reading, they'll have to ride fish and wear tutus.

So the knights rode into the hills to the dragon's cave.

"Dragon, come fight!" shouted Sir Wilbur. From inside the cave came a mighty

RRRRROARRR!!!

They prepared to face . . . the dragon.

Now, Ned and I admire how well you read. But the story will be ruined if you turn the page right now. So please don't.

EEEEEEK!

Oops!

The dragon's still in the shower. He didn't think he'd be needed this soon.

But you turned the page. That means we need a dragon. And the best Ned could find was this pretzel.

So Sir Wilbur and his knights rode their trusty fish into battle with the pretzel.

After a fierce fight, the pretzel was defeated. At the celebration the king said, "For your second task, you must build a mighty wall around my castle."

Sir Wilbur said, "It shall be done."

Wait, for Ned's sake. Making walls takes time, hard work, and . . .

Why do you keep turning the page? I asked you nicely.
Poor Ned had to build the walls with the first thing he could find—grape Popsicles.

Sir Wilbur presented the king with mighty purple walls. "Very well," said the king, "but for the third and final task, you must fill my castle moat with the meanest creature in the sea."

Sir Wilbur said, "It shall be done."

Don't turn the page until tomorrow.
Ned needs time to go to the ocean, get a boat, and catch the most terrifying creature anyone has ever seen . . .

This is Ned's dog, Trevor. With a shark fin tied to his head. That's the closest Ned could get to a sea creature.

Look, we're trying to tell a good story, but you're reading too fast.

ir Wilbur said, "Your Pie-ness, I've given you the fiercest shark-dog around. I've completed your three tasks. I wish to wed your daughter."

"Never!" cried the king. "And now that I'm protected by walls and a moat, no one can take her pies from me!" And he threw all the knights out of the castle onto their tutus.

Actually, you can turn this page.
Ned spent all night on the next picture.

Thank you.

Later that night, an enormous pie appeared at the castle gates. "Bring it inside for my breakfast tomorrow," the king ordered. So his guards dragged the pie into the castle. But this was no ordinary pie. Sir Wilbur's men had baked it and hidden him inside.

And when everyone was asleep, Sir Wilbur pulled himself free.

Meanwhile, in her tower, the princess was getting bored waiting to be rescued. Suddenly a voice cried, "Never fear! Sir Wilbur's here!"

She turned and saw him standing on a ladder outside her window.

"My hero!" said the princess.

Oops! Ned worked on that pie so much, he's fallen behind. He's hammer-and-nailing furiously. But it's really important that you DON'T TURN THE PAGE! Trust me.

Because Sir Wilbur leaped in to meet the princess and . . .

AAAAAGGH!

He fell through the hole in the floor that Ned couldn't fix. Because you turned the page. I hope you're happy.

Down and down Sir Wilbur fell until SPLAT! He landed in the king's smelly dungeon.

The princess was getting mad. "I'll never get rescued at this rate! I'll just have to do it myself."

So she climbed down the ladder and ran toward
the forest to find Sir Wilbur's knights. . . .

Please. Ned's exhausted. . . . The forest isn't ready. Plus the
knights aren't here. They're off eating lunch. No one thought
you'd read this quickly.
So you CAN'T go on, right?

This is getting ridiculous.

Ned had to dress monkeys in the knights' costumes. And we'll pretend those crayons are trees.

The princess told the monkey-knights, "The king has Sir Wilbur imprisoned. Bring me a fish and a sword, and together we can save him!"

"Ooh! Ooh!" cried the monkeys. In monkey language, that means, "Hurrah! Fetch her a fish and a banana-sword!"

STOP.
Stop. Right. Now.
I refuse to let you turn this page.

Fine.
But just so you know, Ned has run out
of fish. The only thing left is this snail.

So the princess led the monkey-knights veeerrry slooowly into battle. And not just any battle, either, but the biggest, most exciting battle any storybook has ever seen!

This is your final warning.

The next page won't be ready for four or five weeks. So put the book down and come back then. Okay?

Pretty please?

"Oh no . . . , " said Ned.

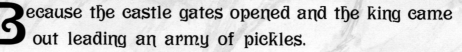

Because the castle gates opened and the king came out leading an army of pickles.

"You're outnumbered," said the king. "Surrender!"

"Never!" The princess raised her banana and cried, "CHAAARGE!"

Suddenly a flock of pretzels flew down and melted the Popsicle walls into a rushing river that swept the pickles away and WHACK! the princess knocked the king into the moat and then . . .

Ned quit!

He can't take it anymore.
We'll have to finish without
his help.

"Help!" yelled the king. "Eww! Why won't someone help me?"
Trevor was holding him down, slobbering on his doughnut-
covered head. But with Trevor distracted, the princess crossed the
moat unharmed.

Then, she rescued Sir Wilbur.

And together the princess and Sir Wilbur rode
her snail very slowly into the half-painted sunset.

Now we've run out of the letter *E*.
Good thing for all of us that this is . . .

TH ND.

KERSHAW COUNTY LIBRARY

3 3255 00275 7764

J
398.2
Len

Lendler, Ian.

An undone fairy
tale.

OCT   2009

$15.95

DATE			

KERSHAW COUNTY LIBRARY WITHDRAWN
632 W. DeKalb St. Suite 109
Camden, South Carolina 29020

BAKER & TAYLOR